Dear
Mr. President ™

OTHER DEAR MR. PRESIDENT™ BOOKS

Thomas Jefferson
Letters from a Philadelphia Bookwor
By Jennifer Armstrong

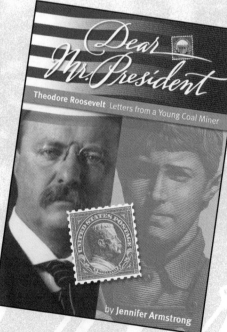

Theodore Roosevelt
Letters from a Young Coal Miner
By Jennifer Armstrong

Abraham Lincoln
Letters from a Slave Girl
by **Andrea Davis Pinkney**

Franklin Delano Roosevelt
Letters from a Mill Town Girl
by **Elizabeth Winthrop**

READ YOUR WAY INTO THE PAST...

History comes alive in this collection of fictitious letters exchanged between President John Quincy Adams and William Pratt—the twelve-year-old son of a cotton plantation owner. But there is much more to discover.

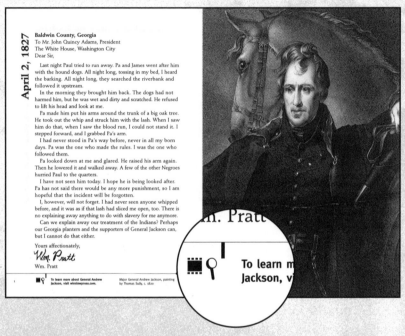

Baldwin County, Georgia

April 2, 1827

To Mr. John Quincy Adams, President
The White House, Washington City

Dear Sir,

Last night Paul tried to run away. Pa and James went after him with the hound dogs. All night long, tossing in my bed, I heard the barking. All night long, they searched the riverbank and followed it upstream.

In the morning they brought him back. The dogs had not harmed him, but he was wet and dirty and scratched. He refused to lift his head and look at me.

Pa made him put his arms around the trunk of a big oak tree. He took out the whip and struck him with the lash. When I saw him do that, when I saw the blood run, I could not stand it. I stepped forward, and I grabbed Pa's arm.

I had never stood in Pa's way before, never in all my born days. Pa was the one who made the rules. I was the one who followed them.

Pa looked down at me and glared. He raised his arm again. Then he lowered it and walked away. A few of the other Negroes hurried Paul to the quarters.

I have not seen him today. I hope he is being looked after. Pa has not said there would be any more punishment, so I am hopeful that the incident will be forgotten.

I, however, will not forget. I had never seen anyone whipped before, and it was as if that lash had sliced me open, too. There is no explaining away anything to do with slavery for me anymore.

Can we explain away our treatment of the Indians? Perhaps our Georgia planters and the supporters of General Jackson can, but I cannot do that either.

Yours affectionately,

Wm. Pratt
Wm. Pratt

To learn more about General Andrew Jackson, visit winslowpress.com.

Major General Andrew Jackson, painting by Thomas Sully, c. 1820

Throughout the book, there is a series of "interactive footnotes" called Web prompts leading the reader to our virtual library at **winslowpress.com**. Once there they will find out more about many of the topics discussed in the letters of the book as well as links for further exploration, pictures, and even audio and video clips.

Icons next to each footnote in the book let readers know what kinds of additional resources they will find when they visit the Web site.

PHOTOGRAPHS

VIDEO CLIPS

AUDIO CLIPS

LINKS

CLICK TO MAKE IT COME ALIVE AT WINSLOWPRESS.COM

VISIT THE DEAR MR.
PRESIDENT WEB SITE
AT WINSLOWPRESS.COM

CLICK ON THE COVER
OF THE BOOK YOU
WANT TO EXPLORE.

CHOOSE FROM THE
LIST OF WEB PROMPTS
FROM THE BOOK.

READ, WATCH, AND LISTEN AS THE
TOPICS UNFOLD BEFORE YOUR EYES.

Dear Mr. President ™

Dear Mr. President™

John Quincy Adams
Letters from a Southern Planter's Son

by Steven Kroll

WINSLOW PRESS

New York

Discover *Dear Mr. President*'s™ interactive Web site with worldwide
links, games, activities, and more at **winslowpress.com**

Attempting to create a voice for John Quincy Adams, I have occasionally used words and phrases taken from his diary, *The Memoirs of John Quincy Adams*, volumes 6 and 7, edited by Charles Francis Adams. Philadelphia: J.B. Lippincott Co., 1875.

I would like to thank E. Lorene Flanders, Assistant Director for Instruction and Reference Services, Ina Dillard Russell Library, Georgia College & State University, Milledgeville, Georgia, for all her help and support.

Winslow Press wished to acknowledge the Library of Congress for the photographs and illustrations in this book.

DEAR MR. PRESIDENT™ and the DEAR MR. PRESIDENT™ logo are registered trademarks of Winslow Press.

Special thanks to R. Sean Wilentz, Dayton-Stockton Professor of History, and Director, Program in American Studies, Princeton University, for evaluating the manuscript.

Library of Congress Cataloging-in-Publication Data
Kroll, Steven.
John Quincy Adams: letters from a southern planter's son / by Steven Kroll.
p. cm.
Includes bibliographical references and index.
Summary: Between 1825 and 1827, twelve-year-old William Pratt, who lives in Georgia, corresponds with President John Quincy Adams, discussing what he feels is an unjust treaty with the Creek Indians, Mr. Adams's close election and problems as president, slavery, education, and more.
ISBN: 1-890817-93-7
1. Adams, John Quincy, 1767-1848—Juvenile Fiction. [1. Adams, John Quincy, 1767-1848—Fiction. 2. United States—History—1825-1829—Fiction. 3. Creek Indians—Government relations—Fiction. 4. Indians of North America—Government relations—Fiction. 5. Letters—Fiction.] I. Title. II. Series.

PZ7.K9225 Jo 2001
[Fic]—dc21
2001017686

Creative Director: Bretton Clark
Book
Designer: Victoria Stehl
Editor: Margery Cuyler

Web site
Designer: Patricia Espinosa
Programming: John Fontana
Editor: Laura Harris

Cover illustration: Mark Summers

Printed in Belgium
First edition, October 2001

1 3 5 7 9 10 8 6 4 2

WINSLOW PRESS

115 East 23RD Street 10TH Floor
New York, NY 10010

Discover *Dear Mr. President's* ™ interactive Web site with worldwide links, games, activities, and more at **winslowpress.com**

For Kathleen

A Note from the Publisher

This book is the fifth in the *Dear Mr. President* ™ series. The text is in the form of letters exchanged between President John Quincy Adams and a twelve-year-old boy, William Pratt. Although the letters are fictional, the information in them is based on meticulous research. In order to capture President Adams's personality and the voice of the youth of that time, the author relied on such books as *John Quincy Adams* by Lynn Hudson Parsons, *Milledgeville: Georgia's Antebellum Capital* by James C. Bonner, and *The Diary of John Quincy Adams*, 1794-1845.

The actual treaties mentioned in the book were found at the following Web site: http://www.cuioq.uga.edu/projects/gainfo/creektre.htm/washing2.htm. A list of recommended reading is found on page107.

It is our hope that the *Dear Mr. President* ™ books, portraying issues from other eras, will provide readers with valuable insights into important moments in American history. Each title, written by a skilled author, is further enhanced by interactive footnotes, games, activities, and links, with detailed historical information at the book's own Web site in our virtual library, winslowpress.com.

By offering you a rich reading experience coupled with our interactive Web site, we encourage you to embrace the future with what is best from the past.

Diane F. Kessenich, CEO and Publisher, Winslow Press

West Front of the Capitol of the United States, watercolor, 1824

Dear Mr. President,

Yours respectfully,

William Pratt

Dear Master Pratt,

Your servant,

J. Q. Adams

Introduction

In America in the mid-1820s, southern planters were growing cotton, and the workers they were using were Negro slaves. As the fields wore out and more land was needed, the planters headed farther west, seeking new opportunities and greater profits.

In Georgia, however, a planter could not just sweep across the state, buying up all the rich land he wanted. Some of that land belonged to the Creek Indians, and they were not about to give it up after having lived on it for hundreds of years.

Soon after taking office in 1825, President John Quincy Adams signed and ratified a treaty negotiated with the Creeks. That treaty, the Treaty of Indian Springs, granted all Creek Indian lands to the state of Georgia.

It had been approved by a wide margin in the previous Senate, but the treaty was a fraud. The Creek chiefs who signed it were unauthorized and had been bribed. The two government commissioners, both from Georgia, had encouraged the signing in order to grab the land.

President Adams had only recently been chosen president by the House of Representatives, after an election in which no candidate had won a majority. He had difficult choices to make, and supporters of General Andrew Jackson, the man he had finally beaten, the old Indian fighter himself, were already yapping at his heels.

Imagine a boy named William Pratt, the son of a plantation owner in remote central Georgia. His life was privileged, but not as privileged as those who lived on much larger plantations. He believed that the Treaty of Indian Springs was wrong and that the Creeks should be allowed to keep their land. Imagine that William Pratt wrote to John Quincy Adams, who became the sixth president of the United States on March 4, 1825.

Hoeing on a cotton plantation, sketch by A.R. Waud, printed in *Harper's Weekly*, 1867

Baldwin County, Georgia
To Mr. John Quincy Adams, President
The White House, Washington City
Dear Sir,

I am twelve years old. My father owns a cotton plantation here in Baldwin County, just outside of Milledgeville. Milledgeville, as you will know, is our capital city here in Georgia.

You will not know that our house rests on a rise overlooking the Oconee River. A lot of the houses out here are just log cabins, with one room or maybe two with some clay stuck in between the cracks. Our house is real nice. It's not fancy, but it's got two stories and clapboards all over it. Pa's not one of the richest planters here, but we do own twenty slaves.

I am writing to send my congratulations on your victory, Mr. President, sir. I, for one, am very happy you are in the White House. You seem like a man with principles and education, the kind of man I would want to be. You know, a lot of people here in Georgia do not share that view. They favored General Jackson. They said he was a war hero and more like common folk. They said he was from Tennessee and a tough Indian fighter, too.

I do not trust General Jackson at all. I think he is a brute whose only interest is himself, but if you will forgive me, there is something I need to ask you.

Last year, I saw a Creek Indian held up at gunpoint and robbed on the street in Milledgeville. No one came to his aid. No one pursued the thieves. Afterward, he just stood there, looking helpless and confused. I felt so sorry, but there was nothing I could do.

Now I have learned that about two weeks ago, you signed a treaty with the Creek Indians called the Treaty of Indian

To learn more about the Treaty of Indian Springs, visit winslowpress.com.

A house in Milledgeville, Georgia, 1830

Springs. It said that the Creeks would give up all their land here in Georgia. They would move to an equal amount of land west of the Mississippi River and receive a bonus of $400,000.

Pa thinks this is an excellent agreement. Now more planters will be able to grow cotton on the Creeks' rich land, but to me your action is like what happened to the Indian on the street. I do not think it is fair at all.

I know there have been treaties with the Indians in the past and the government has been wanting to move them west, but why is it not possible for the Creeks to be left alone? Why can they not stay where they have lived for hundreds of years? Do they not have rights like us?

Yours respectfully,

Wm. Pratt

Wm. Pratt

The White House

To Master William Pratt
Baldwin County, Georgia
Dear Master Pratt,

I must thank you for your congratulations and for your comments about my character. My hope is that the people of this great country will come to share your view. During my Inaugural Address, recognizing that I had been chosen president by the House of Representatives rather than the will of the people, I was deeply concerned by the antagonism I felt around me. The assumption that Mr. Clay had handed his votes to me because I agreed to make him secretary of state, that there was a "corrupt bargain" between us, is false, but no one will believe that. My acts as president will have to confirm my worth, and I have begun with my appointments. Without regard for politics, I have renominated every person against whom there was no complaint. Mr. Monroe, my predecessor, always acted on this principle, and I have followed suit.

You asked me about the Treaty of Indian Springs, and I will do my best to respond. My attitude toward the Indians has gone through changes over the years. I began by thinking that we as Europeans had the right to take over aboriginal lands. Now I think the government is responsible for protecting the Indians against violations of their treaty rights.

The Treaty of Indian Springs appeared to acknowledge rights given to the state of Georgia in the treaty of Fort Wilkinson, signed in 1802. The new treaty was on my desk when I took office, and I signed and ratified it because the outgoing Senate's vote of approval had been by a wide margin.

April 15, 1825

To learn more about the election of 1824, visit winslowpress.com.

Secretary of State Henry Clay

Colonel John Crowell, the United States Indian agent responsible for the welfare of the Creeks in the area, has raised strong objections of his own. I am looking into the matter further.

Your humble servant,

J. Q. Adams

John Quincy Adams

May 7, 1825

Baldwin County, Georgia
To Mr. John Quincy Adams, President
The White House, Washington City
Dear Sir,

With all due respect, sir, the Treaty of Indian Springs is a cheat. Pa has told me the details. It was signed by William McIntosh, the main chief of the Lower Creek tribes, and seven lesser chiefs. The Creek Nation has forty-six towns. Those chiefs represented only eight and had no business speaking for the Upper Creeks at all. The two commissioners involved were from Georgia. They encouraged the signing because they wanted the land.

What a terrible injustice, and now there has been an even more terrible result. Last week, four hundred angry Upper Creeks swooped down on Chief McIntosh's plantation. They burned it and shot him dead in front of his home. Then they stabbed him.

As if this were not enough, our Governor Troup, who seems to me like a crazy man, continues to insist that the treaty is valid and must stand. He is a first cousin of Chief McIntosh, though not part Indian himself, and he even wants the Creeks' land to be surveyed for sale to settlers before the September 1, 1826 deadline specified by the treaty.

I reckon this is a real bad state of affairs, what with Creek turning against Creek and Governor Troup acting in such bad faith.

Pa has told me that the Creeks live in permanent villages, in huts around a plaza where they have dancing and religious ceremonies. He also says they have become more than

To learn more about the tribes of the Creek Nation, visit winslowpress.com.

Creek chief William McIntosh

passable farmers. Why should they not be allowed to keep their villages? Can you do nothing for them?

Forgive me for asking so many questions, but I figure that you, being president, can give me some truthful answers.

Yours respectfully,

Wm. Pratt

Wm. Pratt

The White House
To Master William Pratt
Baldwin County, Georgia
Dear Master Pratt,

Your letter arrived on May 15, the same day that Chilly McIntosh and three other Lower Creek Indians visited my office here in Washington. Chilly is the son of Chief McIntosh and favors the sale of the land to Georgia. He escaped the attack on the McIntosh plantation and was here to protest it and to present me with a letter from your Governor Troup. As you would imagine, the letter was angry. It defended the treaty. It accused Agent Crowell, who had opposed the treaty from the beginning, with instigating the massacre. It vowed revenge. I was deeply distressed by the governor's letter, as I was by yours. I advised Chilly that he call on Secretary of War Barbour the next day.

Chilly did so and leveled specific charges against Agent Crowell. He also mentioned a protection clause in the Treaty of Indian Springs that had been violated. It is thought that the Creeks as a nation might begin a war in Georgia and that Governor Troup could encourage such a war to aid in their removal. Secretary Barbour has ordered Major General Edmund Gaines to repair to Creek Territory and await instructions. The secretary has sent a special agent, Timothy Andrews, to investigate. I have instructed General Gaines to warn Governor Troup to postpone the surveying of the Territory.

It has begun to become clear that Agent Crowell is not at fault and that a whole series of mistakes, beginning with the selection of the two Georgians as commissioners and concluding with the Senate's and my carelessness, contributed to the ratifying of the Treaty of Indian Springs. Just what is to be done remains uncertain, but I wanted you to know

To learn more about
William McIntosh, visit
winslowpress.com.

that the matter is of great concern, as much for all of us in Washington as it is for you in Georgia.

I am weighed down by many obligations. I have been working to secure approval for a representative to the conference of Latin American republics in Panama and trying to choose a vessel to protect our fisheries off the coasts of Maine and New Brunswick. However, I have entered this new course of life, specially responsible to God, to my country, and to mankind, and I have intensely felt the need to devote all my time and all my faculties to the discharge of my duties.

Your servant,

J. Q. Adams

J. Q. Adams

President John Quincy Adams, painted by Thomas Sully, 1826

Baldwin County, Georgia

To Mr. John Quincy Adams, President
The White House, Washington City
Dear Sir,

Pa says Governor Troup is right. The treaty should stand even if it was not done the way it should have been. The Creeks should give up their land and move so white settlers can buy that land in a lottery.

Pa and I have been quarreling about this. Our plantation is four hundred and five acres that Pa bought in a lottery back before I was born, but I do not think that makes forcing the Indians off their land all right. I have also learned that the government had offered Chief McIntosh land on the Arkansas River if he left Georgia. He had planned to go look at it soon after signing the treaty. I do not think that is right either. The government should not be bribing anyone just so they can get what they want.

Pa says I am too young to have these opinions and that I should calm down and listen to him, but I am just glad that you, Mr. President, in the White House, are trying to see that justice is done.

Soon after my last letter, school let out for the month of May. We are back at our desks now, and I will keep my musings about vacation for my next letter. In the meantime, knowing of your interest in education, I will attempt to convey some thoughts about school.

We live a mile away. Each morning, my sister Sarah, who is ten, and I walk that distance, accompanied by our Negro, Paul. He stays long enough to see that we are settled, then goes back to our plantation and returns for us at four to see us home.

To learn more about
land sold by lottery,
visit winslowpress.com.

Our school is a long, one-room log building. It has a big chimney at one end and many benches inside. Our teacher's name is Mr. McAllister. He is very fat and rides to school on an old swaybacked horse. Some of the children make fun of him, but he is a very good teacher, even though he never minds using a hickory switch when we misbehave. Most of the time we call him "Old Mac."

School starts at eight o'clock. At my level, we ended the term studying Greek and Latin, algebra, history, and the French language. When the weather warmed up, the boys did their lessons outside. I liked that a great deal, and I liked writing on the slate Pa bought me in town.

Yours respectfully,

Wm. Pratt

Wm. Pratt

Georgia cotton crop

The White House
To Master William Pratt
Baldwin County, Georgia
Dear Master Pratt,

I am pleased to learn of your rising early, always a good practice, and walking a mile to school with your sister. Walking has always been a part of my life, too, and it remains so, though now that the hot weather is upon us, my exercise regimen has changed. I no longer take my customary walk between four and six in the evening. Instead, between the hours of seven and nine in the morning, I can be found bathing and swimming in the Potomac.

I continue to rise at about five and read two chapters of the Bible, complete with commentary, followed by the morning newspapers and public papers from the several departments. Then my swim, followed by breakfast, sometimes with Mrs. Adams, for an hour, from nine to ten, and afterward an endless succession of visitors, including heads of departments, from eleven till between four and five o'clock. Dinner is from half-past five to seven, and in the evening, I am either in my chamber or wasting my time in idleness or at the billiard table. I retire at about eleven.

It is refreshing to know of your own interest in education. I tried very hard to kindle that interest in my own three sons but have enjoyed little success. Now that you have begun the study of Greek and Latin, you should discover the Latin orations of Cicero, a great opponent of tyranny.

Your servant,

John Quincy Adams

To learn more about Cicero, visit winslowpress.com.

A Latin text, decorated with a picture of Cicero

Marci Tulij Ciceronis Arpinatis, consulisq̃. romani, ac oratoru maximi Ad M. Tulliu Ciceronem filiu suu. Officio᷒ liber incipit. Prefacio generalis in libros omnes.

Quanq̃ te marce fili, annum iam audietem cratippu, idq̃ athenis, abundare oportet, preceptis, institutisq̃ phie, ppt summa doctoris auctate, et urbis, quo᷒ alteru te scietia augere potest, altera exeplis. tame ut ipe, ad mea utilitate semp cu grecis latina coiuxi, neq̃ id in phia solu, sed etiaz in dicedi exercitatione feci, id tibi censeo faciendu, ut par sis in utriusq̃ o᷒omis facultate. Qua quide ad re, nos ut videmur, magnu adiumetu attulimus homib̃ nris, ut non modo greca᷒ lia᷒ rudes, sed etiam docti, aliquantu se arbitrent adeptos, et ad discendu et ad iudicadu. Quaobre disces tu quide a pricipe huius etatis pho᷒, et disces quadiu voles, tadiu autez velle debebis, quoad te quatii pficias no penitebit. Sed tame nra leges, no multu a peripatheticis dissidentia, q̃m utriq̃ socratici z platonici volumus esse.

Baldwin County, Georgia
To Mr. John Quincy Adams, President
The White House, Washington City
Dear Sir,

Thanks for your letter and for describing the activities in your day. You sound very busy! I had said that I would tell you about my vacation, so I will.

Many wealthy plantation owners in Georgia take their families away to summer colonies for the entire planting season, leaving their slaves to do the work. They are trying to escape the heat and the dangers of malaria. Their children continue to go to school wherever they are, though their vacation months, like ours, are May and December.

My family does not go away because we cannot afford it. In addition, malaria has not been a problem recently in Baldwin County. So last May, when school was out, I spent some time at the creek near our house.

Paul came along. He goes everywhere with me, though we do not share much conversation. He is like my shadow.

Some days we just eased our way around in the rowboat. Other days we went out fishing or swimming. Paul was real good at diving off the boat, but I liked swimming underwater best.

As I recall my time at the creek, I think about you swimming in the Potomac River. Is that not a dangerous thing to do? Do you not encounter mean currents in that river that could sweep you away? Are you sure you are safe? Forgive me, Mr. President, but I worry about you.

Other times during vacation, Paul and I went hunting. Pa let us use the shotgun and the rifle as long as we were real careful. He showed us how to use them both three years ago and made us promise we would not do anything untoward.

When we go into the woods with the guns, I cannot say I enjoy myself. I once shot a squirrel, but it made me sick to my stomach. If I have the opportunity to shoot a deer, I aim the other way. I think that hunting is a practice I will choose not to pursue in the future.

People out here carry guns and fight duels. It is hard for me to imagine doing either one.

Mr. President, I know you will be glad to learn that most days when school was out, Pa got me up at six. We made a tour of the plantation together, checking on how the Negroes were weeding the cotton and the corn and how the hogs and chickens were doing. We looked into the Negroes' row of log cabins to make sure nothing was amiss. They are right behind our house and very well kept. In the afternoon we went over the accounts, discussing everything from the cost of cotton seed to what it takes to provide the Negroes with two suits of clothing and a pair of shoes each year, plus their monthly allowances of corn, pork, and molasses. Pa wants me to grow up to be just like him. He also says he wants me to be a very rich planter and have more slaves than he has.

I have asked Mr. McAllister about that fellow Cicero. He will inquire at the bookstore in Milledgeville. If he has no luck there, he will ask again when next he is in Augusta.

Yours respectfully,

Wm. Pratt

Wm. Pratt

Background: A child in front of a slave cabin

To learn more about the lives of slaves, visit winslowpress.com.

33

The White House

To Master William Pratt

Baldwin County, Georgia

Dear Master William,

I am glad to know of your vacation. Your father seems to have kept you from total idleness, and that is not a bad thing. When I was your age, I traveled with my father on missions of diplomacy to France and Holland. It was during our Revolution, a very different time from the present, though I am aware that the supporters of General Jackson would gladly see the overthrow of this Administration tomorrow, if it were possible.

I must confess that your fears about my swimming are not unfounded. Last June 13, I had a very near brush with disaster. I was crossing the river in a canoe with my valet Antoine, intending to swim back. Halfway across, the boat began to leak, and a fresh breeze made it sink even faster. I was forced to jump into the water in my clothes, struggling for life and gasping as I thrashed my way to shore. My carriage had to take us home. Then, just last week, I arrived at my favorite rock, where I customarily remove my clothes, to discover that a clerk in the post office, a man of sixty years of age known to be an excellent swimmer, had drowned.

Since that time, Mrs. Adams would keep me from the Potomac if she could. You, no doubt, would do the same, but I believe that we are in the hands of God and to Him we are indebted for every breath we draw. Periods of swimming are healthful to me in this stifling Washington heat, though my friends would like to tell you that it is the swimming that is responsible for my recent nervous irritability, dejection of spirits, and soreness and pain in my right side. I will try more walking, but not exclusively.

To learn more about JQA's cabinet, visit winslowpress.com.

Governor Troup has sent additional insulting letters to Secretary of War Barbour and myself. My cabinet has now approved a letter from Secretary Barbour, ignoring the insults but making clear that under no circumstances will the survey of Creek Indian lands take place before the proper time. General Gaines has been instructed to use force, if necessary, to uphold this proclamation.

There is no respite from the responsibilities of my office. I have now launched the frigate *Brandywine*, which will take General Lafayette home to France when his triumphal tour of America ends in the fall.

With best wishes,

J. Q. Adams

John Quincy Adams

Secretary of War James Barbour
Background: Great Falls of the Potomac River

Baldwin County, Georgia
To Mr. John Quincy Adams, President
The White House, Washington City
Dear Sir,

I was troubled by the news of your experience on the Potomac River. While it is true that we are in God's hands, you must be more careful of yourself, sir. You are our president, and nothing bad must happen to you.

I was also distressed to learn that you are not feeling well. Ma always says that a strong dose of sassafras tea is good for what ails you, and if I may, I would suggest that you try a cup. Does the White House have a supply of sassafras tea? If not, we will be delighted to send some along.

What is going to happen with Governor Troup? Pa keeps saying he plans on moving ahead with the survey of Creek lands in spite of General Gaines, but I don't think anyone wants to go to war. It seems to me you should get the government to cancel this bad treaty and let the Creeks stay on their land.

You mentioned General Lafayette, and I cannot resist telling you about his visit here. We will never forget that he chose to come to Milledgeville.

It was last March 27. Pa and I rode in early. The roads around town are in terrible condition, nothing but stumps, holes, ruts, and gouges. We had to allow extra time, but we were there when the procession led by Governor Troup met the general's entourage on the east bank of the Oconee River.

Governor Troup and the general rode into town in a barouche drawn by four bay horses. Along with the rest of the crowd, we cheered as they made their way past two lines of Revolutionary War veterans to Government House. Later, the general attended a service at the Methodist Church,

To learn more about the Marquis de Lafayette, visit winslowpress.com. Marquis de Lafayette, who fought on the side of the colonists in the Revolutionary War. In 1824-25, he visited the United States again, by invitation of Congress, and was received as a hero.

a Masonic meeting, and a barbecue, followed by a formal dinner at the Statehouse and a grand ball to which everyone wore his most special finery.

Pa and I were long gone by then, but I wanted you to know that Milledgeville knows how to entertain.

Yours respectfully,

Wm. Pratt

Wm. Pratt

The White House

To Master William Pratt
Baldwin County, Georgia
Dear Master William,

From what you have told me, I would imagine that Milledgeville would be an excellent place to entertain anyone, no less General Lafayette.

Here in Washington City, we have also had the pleasure of entertaining the general. Mrs. Adams considered his stay at the White House an inconvenience but has been stoic about her displeasure. Unfortunately, the entertainments have not been without their perils.

On the 6th of the month, my son John and I, along with several others, escorted General Lafayette on a visit to Mr. James Monroe's estate, Oakhill. We crossed the Potomac bridge, rode to Fairfax Court House, and stayed at a hotel. The next day, six miles from Mr. Monroe's, the crosspiece of the front axle of my carriage snapped off and had to be spliced together. The general and I rode the rest of the way, but the remainder of our party was forced to walk.

A few days later, Mr. Monroe and I accompanied the general to a celebration in Leesburg, Virginia. The heat was so intense, we had a blazing and suffocating afternoon. There were addresses and a public dinner, and Mr. Monroe and I were obliged to share a chamber with two beds in it. Attempting to complete our return, we took the turnpike road, hilly and excessively rough. The most spirited of my four horses collapsed, never again to rise. We then continued over the Georgetown bridge, which is in very bad condition.

The general soon went off to visit Mr. Jefferson and Mr. Madison. When I had breakfast with him recently, I cautioned against his participating in any revolutionary projects in

To learn more about JQA's ideas about internal improvements, visit winslowpress.com.

France. He said that he is sixty-eight years old and must leave revolutions to younger men, but as I recorded in my diary, "there is fire beneath the embers." He will set sail for Le Havre in September.

I am reminded of what you said about the roads in Milledgeville. All over our country, we are in need of internal improvements. It is necessary to build canals and other better means of transportation. These internal improvements are part of my grand scheme, a scheme I will discuss in the Annual Message I must present to Congress in December. Let us hope for a favorable response from the membership.

Meanwhile, Governor Troup has demanded the removal, arrest, and trial of General Gaines. The governor is, as Secretary of War Barbour says, full of "guns, drums, trumpets, blunderbuss, and thunder," but he has also written to the secretary declaring that for the time being, he will not make the threatened survey of Creek Indian lands. At the very least, we seem to have gained a little time.

As for the sassafras tea, the White House larder has been thoroughly ransacked and none discovered. I could not be happier if you would like to send me some.

Your servant,

J. Q. Adams

John Quincy Adams

September 17, 1825

Baldwin County, Georgia
To Mr. John Quincy Adams, President
The White House, Washington City
Dear Sir,

The day after I got your letter, I rustled up some sassafras tea from Mammy Chloe, our cook, and put it in a box. Then I walked up to the stagecoach stand that is two miles south of here. I wanted to be sure the box went out with the mail when the stagecoach came through that afternoon.

As I walked, I noticed all over again how bad the road is. The coaches sometimes tip over, and I have witnessed passengers leaning out the sides to help the vehicles keep their balance. I think I would be even more nervous if I had to ride the coaches often myself, which I do not. But remembering your own difficulties, I can state that stagecoach accidents are one more reason for your internal improvements.

Walking home, I gave more thought to Governor Troup and the Creek Indians. Of course I am happy that the governor will not make the survey yet, but all I can imagine is those poor Creeks in their villages waiting to learn if they will have to move. That does not seem right, and it seems even less right when it is happening because a bunch of greedy white folks want Creek land for growing cotton.

I also thought about cotton and how most of the work of growing it is done by Negro slaves. Pa says he could not run a cotton plantation without slave labor, but with all my thinking about the Indians, I have begun to question the correctness of slavery as well. Although we are real good to our Negroes, what right do we have to own another person just because his skin is a different color from ours? That person should have rights and be free to do as he chooses, just as the Creek Indians should have rights, too.

I got so tangled up in these thoughts, I had to sit myself down under a tree to sort them out.

The next day, Paul and I were down at the creek skipping stones across the water. I asked him if he would like to be free. He looked at me and skipped another stone. He said, "Yeah," and then he looked away. He did not say any more. I think he was worried I might tell Pa.

Yours respectfully,

Wm. Pratt

Wm. Pratt

P.S. I hope you like the tea.

To learn more about cotton plantations, visit winslowpress.com.

Sowing seeds on a cotton plantation, sketch by A.R. Waud, printed in *Harper's Weekly*, 1867

November 4, 1825

The White House
To Master William Pratt
Baldwin County, Georgia
Dear Master William,

Forgive me. In my last letter, I neglected to mention that with the Creek Indian situation temporarily stabilized, I took the opportunity to flee the oppressive heat of Washington City and went to visit at my family home, known as the Old House, in Quincy, Massachusetts. Sacks of mail, most of it official business, were directed to me there, but the system is not a good one and somehow your last letter was not included. I have only now, upon my return, received and read it. I hope you did not think I had forgotten you.

I did enjoy my visit in Quincy. The journey, by carriage and steamboat, takes days and can be stultifying, but once I arrived at the farm, my mood altered. I was elated walking the fields and visiting with my father, who is very frail now but still of good mind. Contrary to my usual feelings, I even appreciated a little public adulation.

Mrs. Adams was ill on the trip back. She does not like returning to what she calls the "great unsocial house." In winter she can never get the rooms warmed enough for congenial entertaining and is often down with a cold or other maladies that confine her to her room.

While away, I spent many hours focusing on my Annual Address. As you have suggested, repairing the roads for the improvement of stagecoach travel will certainly be part of the plan for internal improvements. My sights, however, have risen even higher. I would like to propose a national university, a whole Department of the Interior to handle those internal improvements, and a national astronomical observatory, the

To learn more about the Old House in Quincy, Massachusetts, visit winslowpress.com.

first of many that I would call "light-houses of the skies."
I would like to fund scientific expeditions and establish a
uniform system of weights and measures. Our people deserve
so much, and there is much more on my list.

I have left your most important question for last. Now that
you have made mention of it, I can tell you that I consider that
"peculiar institution" of slavery a moral evil. There is nothing
acceptable about holding another man in bondage, but your
Southern states refuse to abandon the pursuit and wish even
to continue it into the territories. This is the issue that could
divide our Union. I fear for the future of our nation.

On a lighter note, thank you for the tea. It smells horrible
when brewed, but the taste and the effect are beguiling.

Your servant,

J. Q. Adams

John Quincy Adams

The "Old House," The Adams family
residence in Quincy, Massachusetts

To learn more about
JQA's views on slavery,
visit winslowpress.com.

Baldwin County, Georgia
To Mr. John Quincy Adams, President
The White House, Washington City
Dear Sir,

I did not think you had forgotten me. To be honest, I thought my remarks about slavery had in some way offended you and that you would not write to me again. I am grateful that this is not the case and even more grateful that you share my view. In my present situation, there is not a great deal that I can do about this view, but having it, at least, is a start.

I did notice, however, that in your reply you made no mention of the particular rights of the Creek Indians.

Your Annual Message sounds inspired. I got to thinking some more about the internal improvements when I was helping Pa bring the cotton crop into Milledgeville in our wagons. Transporting bales of cotton or any other goods out of Milledgeville is not so easy to do. You would think the Oconee River would be the best way, but the river is treacherous and very difficult to navigate. Steamboats have come, but they have a hard time. Pole boats are the best, but they are slow. Most people hire wagons overland to Darien or Savannah, but that's slow, too, and can be dangerous if you should happen to encounter thieves or bad weather or terrible conditions on the road.

The problem is that the people do not seem to want the government in Washington City to help make transportation better. They want the state of Georgia to take charge, but the state is not about to do that. All I can say is, I hope you succeed.

Yours respectfully,

Wm. Pratt

Wm. Pratt

To learn more about the issues of state versus federal authority, visit winslowpress.com.

A raft that ferried passengers across the Oconee River, Greene County, Georgia

December 4, 1825

The White House
To Master William Pratt
Baldwin County, Georgia
Dear Master William,

A deputation of Creek Indians representing the entire Creek Nation arrived in my office last week. Opothle Yoholo, speaker of the Nation and first chief of the deputation, said they were glad to be here and that others were coming. They had been frightened by recent events and hoped all would be well again.

I said that I, too, had heard things which displeased me, and I expected they would be able to arrange matters with the secretary of war to the satisfaction of all.

Now, it seems, there has been a complication. Based on an earlier meeting with General Gaines and what may have been a misunderstanding on his part, the Indians are saying they do not want to give up all their land in Georgia, that they wish to keep the portion that lies beyond the Chattahoochee River.

I have explained that my interest is in protecting the Creeks' treaty rights and in salvaging the situation. Secretary of War Barbour, who believes we should absorb the Indians into our own system of government and not sign any more treaties with them at all, seems to favor their request for the Chattahoochee boundary.

After my original meeting with the deputation, I held a cabinet meeting, the purpose of which was to share the draft of my Annual Message. There were objections to every part. Only Mr. Rush, secretary of the Treasury, approved nearly the whole.

I understand that many are taking a position against strong, active government, but I remain determined. Tomorrow at noon, my son John, who serves as my private secretary, will bring the message to Congress.

Your servant,

J. Q. Adams

John Quincy Adams

To learn more about the history of the Creek Nation, visit winslowpress.com.

Richard Rush, Secretary of the Treasury

The White House

To Master William Pratt
Baldwin County, Georgia
Dear Master William,

It is barely ten days since I composed my last letter to you, yet I feel compelled to write again. You will have read reports in the newspapers of what has occurred, but since I had given you expectations, I wanted you to hear the cruel truth from me.

The Annual Message has been rebuffed. Friends are saying that because I was not simply rejected outright as the presidential choice of the House of Representatives, I should be optimistic. I am not. Congress, the people, and the press have cast me out.

To my sorrow, it is true. No one wants the federal government to embark upon programs that will give it power over the states, especially in your slaveholding South. In the same spirit, because I chose in my Address to praise the intellectual accomplishments of Europe and criticize the failings of Congress, my time abroad has been turned against me. It does not matter that I helped negotiate the Treaty of Ghent, which ended the War of 1812, or that I served ably as secretary of state. I have been called a monarchist, a man out of sympathy with public opinion.

More contemptible still, my critics have taken the phrase "light-houses of the skies" and jeered at it.

I am writing also to inform you that Chilly McIntosh has reappeared along with ten or twelve other Creek Indians, all claiming to be friendly representatives of the Creek Nation but in truth, I suspect, representing the McIntosh family and the interests of Governor Troup. The superintendent of Indian Affairs lodged them on Pennsylvania

To learn more about JQA's first Annual Message, visit winslowpress.com.

Avenue, but the Georgia delegation to Congress has moved them to a hotel on Capitol Hill, where it is paying their expenses, keeping them away from politicians, and no doubt making certain that they continue to hold the right opinions.

Meanwhile, the principal deputation, led by Opothle Yoholo, wants to see me again before they go. I have said that I will be glad to see them but wish it to be a pleasant, comfortable talk, and hope that there might be a proposition to which we can agree. Now it has become clear that General Gaines did propose the Chattahoochee boundary at his last meeting with the deputation. Needless to say, he had the approval of neither Mr. Barbour nor myself, but with the proposal having been placed on the table, we are obligated to consider it seriously.

I hope you will not be quick to condemn the politics and the tortuousness of the events surrounding the resolution of this matter. Would that such a resolution be simply a question of doing to others as one would be done by, a maxim close to my heart. Unfortunately, that is seldom the case. The complications are invariably greater.

At this time of year, my routine is slightly different from before. I rise between five and six and walk by the light of the moon and stars (or none) about four miles. Usually I return home in time to see the sun rise over the East Room of the White House. Then I light the fire, read my Bible, and begin the day. With Mrs. Adams seldom in evidence, I feel the want of companionship.

I send you best wishes for the holidays.

Your servant,

J. Q. A.

JQA

Two unidentified Creek chiefs

December 24, 1825

Baldwin County, Georgia
To Mr. John Quincy Adams, President
The White House, Washington City
Dear Sir,

I was honored to receive two letters from you in such a short time. That a man as important as yourself should wish to write to me so often fills me with pride.

I also feel badly for you. Those internal improvements you mentioned were a real good idea for the country. I bet some day they will get done, even if you do not get to do them. All those other suggestions were good, too, and it is wrong that you were attacked for them. You do not seem to me like a man who would want to be a king.

I see you as a man of virtue and high-mindedness. I do not think many kings are like that.

I continue to be concerned about what is happening with the Creek Indians. I think I understand what you are saying about the politics, but why is it not possible for you simply to void the treaty and let the Creeks keep their land? Why are they negotiating for just a little piece of what is theirs?

In spite of your reservations, why is this not a question of doing to others as one would be done by, a passage that, I am certain, comes from the Bible?

I am not as familiar with the Bible as you are, sir. We are not serious Bible readers or churchgoers out here in the country. Many of us, according to the Methodist circuit riders, are downright sinful and ungodly. Sometimes, when Sarah and I were little, Ma read us stories from the Bible before we went to sleep, but that is about as close as we ever got to such matters. What I am trying to say, though, is that in the present situation, the Bible is likely to be correct and we should follow its teachings.

At least Governor Troup seems to have quieted down for a while. I reckon he is home on his plantation for Christmas.

I am home and glad to be here, but I get worried about your being by yourself. You, sir, are the president of the United States. Anybody you wish to have at your side should be there.

Sometimes, here in the middle of Georgia, I feel real lonesome myself. The plantations are far apart, and often the only children I see besides Sarah and Paul are at school. Besides, people are moving away all the time, trying to stake out those new lands farther west. During Christmas, though, everyone is at home and it's good.

Yours respectfully,

Wm. Pratt

Wm. Pratt

To learn more about Governer George M. Troup, visit winslowpress.com.

Baldwin County, Georgia
To Mr. John Quincy Adams, President
The White House, Washington City
Dear Sir,

I write to share some memories of our Christmas.

Mammy Chloe stood at the hearth in the big open kitchen with all the polished pots and pans on hooks over her head. She slipped turkey and pork and suet pudding onto the long dining room table like magic. We don't have a lot of fancy furnishings, but we do have a whole set of fine French china, and it was all laid out on a white lace tablecloth. Our nearest neighbors, the Hammonds, came over, and they sat at the table with Ma and Pa and Sarah and me. The candles glowed, and everyone was smiling and feeling just fine. After dinner, Ma showed off the new quilt she was working on.

Later on, Pa and I walked down to the quarters to say Merry Christmas. The Negroes had finished their own festive dinner. They had eaten up all the extra pork, corn, and molasses Pa had given them for the holiday. Paul was sitting in a corner surrounded by his family. He and I shared a look. My stomach tightened as I wondered once again why slavery has to be, but it was Christmas and I dwelt on the kinder side.

I hope you are enjoying the holidays.

Yours respectfully,

Wm. Pratt

Wm. Pratt

This etching of a slave cook is an example of the stereotypical way in which slaves were portrayed in the 1800s.

January 30, 1826

The White House
To Master William Pratt
Baldwin County, Georgia
Dear Master William,

Thank you for your good wishes. I did enjoy my holidays
very much. Mrs. Adams and I celebrated here at the White
House with our son John and Mrs. Adams's niece and two
nephews, the orphaned Hellen children. Although Mrs.
Adams continues to remark on the house's shabbiness and
compares its appearance to an almshouse, I find myself
capable of admiring some of Mr. Monroe's elaborate French
furnishings. To raise everyone's spirits, we had a gilded-
bronze and mirrored-glass centerpiece removed from
a cupboard and placed on the dining table. It had seven
mirrored sections and was so tall no one could see across it.

We added to our celebration by performing two of Mrs.
Adams's plays and listening to her strum the harp, which
she does beautifully. Then, on New Year's Day, there was
the usual visitation between noon and three o'clock. A group
amounting to between two and three thousand persons came,
including the greater portion of both houses of Congress. I
was grateful that it did not last longer than three hours,
although for a moment I felt unusually popular.

Negotiations with the Creek Indians have continued all during
this month, and there was much discussion in the cabinet.
Secretary of War Barbour returned to his view that the Indians
should be incorporated within the states of the Union and that
it would soon be unavoidably necessary to come to such a system.
Mr. Clay replied that it would be impracticable, that there never
was an Indian who took to civilization. He believes the Indians
are destined to extinction and as a race are not worth preserving.

Mr. Barbour was shocked by this view, as was I, but we were not assembled to eliminate the Indian problem, only to resolve the issue with the Creeks. After the Georgia delegation refused to accept the Chattahoochee line and threatened to support General Jackson in the next election if they were not granted the entire territory, Mr. Barbour thought momentarily that if Mr. Clay was right, we should yield. You will be pleased to know that I refused, saying that we could not yield to Georgia without great injustice and that politics and General Jackson had nothing to do with the matter.

The result is that we have a new treaty, the Treaty of Washington, signed at the War Department on January 24. With it, the members of the Creek Nation have accepted as their boundary a more western branch of the Chattahoochee River and will have until January 1, 1827, to leave the remainder of their land. Tomorrow I will send this treaty to the Senate, replacing the invalid Treaty of Indian Springs. The McIntosh delegation, now officially representing the friends and followers of Chief William McIntosh, did not participate, but will sign a separate document to be annexed to the treaty. That document will grant them their own land west of the Mississippi.

Ever and sincerely yours,

J. 2. Adams

J. Q. Adams

P.S. "Do unto others as one would be done by" comes from the New Testament and is taken from two passages, Matthew 7:12 and Luke 6:31.

February 17, 1826

Baldwin County, Georgia
To Mr. John Quincy Adams, President
The White House, Washington City
Dear Sir,

I do not understand. The government signed a treaty with the Creek Indians that everyone admits was plumb wrong. The government has now spent months negotiating to right that wrong, but is not the result almost as bad as before? The Creeks still have to move. They still have to give up their land. They just won't have to give up absolutely all of it.

Where is the justice you said you wanted for these people? You may have protected their treaty rights, but you have not protected them.

I think I sound angry with you, sir. I am not. I am sad. I had hoped you would be able to do something for the Creeks, but I realize nothing is as simple as that. Pa and Governor Troup are still saying that Georgia should have all the land. I should not be surprised that a whole bunch of people believe that.

You sound tired in your letter. I know there is very little unspoken-for time in the White House, but try, if you can, to get some rest the way you did over the holidays.

I am plumb tired myself these days. I have been helping our Negroes clear the acreage in the northernmost portion of our land. Paul has shown me how to do this. The brush is cleared with a machete, but with the trees, you strip the bark from around the base of the trunk. Then, next year, when the tree has died, you come back and cut it down.

To learn more about the Treaty of Washington, visit winslowpress.com.

We do more clearing every year, and every year we have more cotton to grow.

I almost forgot to mention that Old Mac was in Augusta and found the orations by that fellow Cicero. I have been trying to read them, but they are tough going. My Latin is in much need of improvement.

Yours respectfully,

Wm. Pratt

Wm. Pratt

April 28, 1826

The White House
To Master William Pratt
Baldwin County, Georgia
Dear Master William,

I must apologize for the length of time it has taken for me to reply to your last letter. This past winter has been spent in a nearly constant debate with Congress over the sending of what has turned out to be two representatives to that conference in Panama, sponsored by the new Latin American republics. There are many international issues I feel should be discussed at the conference, but the one scheduled to be raised that has had Congress in turmoil concerns the suppression of the slave trade. To your southern bloc in the Senate, even the discussion of such an issue threatens the continuance of slavery in our country, and they and others have created so many delays and disruptions, I cannot even be certain that Mr. Anderson and Mr. Sergeant, the representatives we have chosen, will be allowed to go.

To make matters worse, a half-mad congressman, John Randolph of Roanoke, recently gave an unpardonable speech attacking me and my administration under the guise of opposing the conference. Mr. Clay was so incensed by what was said about him that he was forced to challenge Mr. Randolph to a duel. Fortunately, the only damage was to the congressman's coat.

These details of ill feeling will make you aware that there are duels in Washington City as well as in Milledgeville, but I hope that they will also make you aware that not everything we do here is as straightforward as we would wish. I recognize your feelings for the Creek Indians and their plight. I am more and more apt to share those feelings myself, but the issues involved in the matter have less to do with feelings than with what government can and cannot do.

This is not a monarchy. Just as with the representatives to the Panama conference, I cannot alter the picture with a sweep of my hand. I must have support from Congress, and Congress is made up of representatives from the states, which, as you know, like to decide things for themselves and are resentful when the federal government attempts to interfere. In this case, the Georgia delegation, inflamed by Governor Troup and the supporters of General Jackson, seems to have swayed Congress to take up their cause.

There is some time before the Creeks must move. Perhaps that time will make a difference.

I am interested, however, that Secretary of War Barbour has come up with his own alternative. He has written a letter to the chairman of the Committee on Indian Affairs of the House of Representatives. In this letter, he has given up the idea of incorporating the Indians into the states where they reside. He proposes to transplant them as individuals, not tribes, west of the Mississippi or west of lakes Michigan and Huron. There, they will live under a territorial government maintained by the United States.

Such a plan, I realize, does not in any way meet your concerns. From my less clearly defined perspective, it has merit but is also impracticable.

Your servant,

J. Q. Adams

John Quincy Adams

P.S. Continue your reading of Cicero. Your Latin will improve.

To learn more about the duel between Henry Clay and John Randolph, visit winslowpress.com.

Baldwin County, Georgia
To Mr. John Quincy Adams, President
The White House, Washington City
Dear Sir,

I have been off traveling. Pa had got to thinking that he could be interested in buying some of that Creek land when it finally came up for sale. He was worried that some of our fields were near played out for cotton.

Anyway, vacation came, and Pa asked if I would accompany him to look at the land. I do not need to tell you how I felt about Pa even considering such a purchase, but it would not have been seemly to refuse him. So Paul helped me polish my tack and my boots, and together we groomed my favorite chestnut mare, Belle.

Pa and I set off down the Federal Road, which runs through Milledgeville and crosses the Ocmulgee and Flint rivers before reaching the Chattahoochee at Fort Mitchell, our final destination. We could have headed on into Alabama, but Pa did not want to spend more than a week away. He knew that Ma, as usual, would be looking after the Negroes and that James, our Negro driver, would be taking charge of work in the fields. He simply did not like being away for too long.

Even though I did not much care for the reasons behind our journey, I liked being out and traveling. I liked riding Belle, who was smooth as butter to handle, and I liked spending time alone with Pa, but the Federal Road was in even worse condition than the roads around Milledgeville. We were continually dodging fissures, roots, and sand patches. Anyone interested in pursuing your internal improvements would do well to start with that road.

Yet for me the trip became more unpleasant with the approach of each stream and river. At every one, there were Indians in charge of a bridge or a ferry, and although I found nothing wrong in that, the Indians were overcharging on the tolls. As someone who has spoken out for the Indians, I was embarrassed by the overcharging, but Pa just paid the money.

He was no less indifferent when we passed Indian villages or colorfully dressed Indians on the road. I tried to be the same, but that was hard when I discovered that some of the Indians had slaves.

Indians, who share so few rights in our great country, have taken away the rights of Negroes! Where does the injustice end?

Most of the people we met on our way were families bound for Alabama. Their belongings were bundled onto wagons. They had children, and many had slaves of their own. We rode on by, admiring the landscape around us, from the violets to the irises to the gorgeous wild azaleas with their globe of blossoms bigger than somebody's hand.

At night, we stayed in taverns and at stagecoach stands. The stands had more space and real beds instead of pine slabs with dried cowhide covers.

Pa sure looked at a lot of land, but I do not reckon he saw any he wanted to buy.

You will be glad to know that I have been working on my Latin, and there has been a little improvement.

Yours respectfully,

Wm. Pratt

Wm. Pratt

July 27, 1826

Baldwin County, Georgia
To Mr. John Quincy Adams, President
The Old House
Quincy, Massachusetts
Dear Sir,

I read about your father's passing in the newspapers and wanted to send my condolences. I was not certain where to find you, but knowing that events surrounding this sad moment would have brought you to Quincy, I am taking a chance and sending my letter there.

How hard it must be to lose a father, even when he is ninety-one years old and has lived so full a life. No matter how much Pa and I have been quarreling lately, I could not begin to imagine him gone. He is my strength and my support.

My thoughts are with you, and I send words of comfort and cheer.

Yours respectfully,

Wm. Pratt

Wm. Pratt

September 28, 1826

The Old House
Quincy, Massachusetts
To Master William Pratt
Baldwin County, Georgia
My dear William,

It seems that I must again apologize for the tardiness of my reply, this time to the last two letters you have sent me. You were correct. I am in Quincy, where I have found myself overwhelmed by the tasks of putting my father's affairs in order, attending the many services in his honor, and coming to terms with my grief.

The services, both respectful and dignified, have caused me to rethink my religious faith. Never formally a member of my father's church, I have now taken communion there and been comforted, as I was comforted by your kind words. Thank you for them.

The sequence of events leading to my learning of my father's death seems to have been governed by the slowness of our mail delivery.

At the July Fourth celebration in Washington, honoring the fiftieth anniversary of the Declaration of Independence, neither Mr. Jefferson nor my father, both surviving signers of the Declaration, appeared. Both, however, sent their gracious regrets. Then, on July 8, I received the unexpected news that my father was dangerously ill.

The next day was one of the hottest of the summer. At 5 A.M., I set out for Quincy, with my son John, in my carriage with four horses. By the time I reached Waterloo, I was informed that my father had actually died on July Fourth.

"Funeral Thoughts Excited by the Death of John Adams and Thomas Jefferson," published soon after they died

To learn more about John Adams, visit winslowpress.com.

He had died a few hours after Mr. Jefferson, though he could not have known that. His last words had been "Thomas Jefferson survives." The manner of his dying and its coincidence with Mr. Jefferson's death seem palpable marks of Divine favor. He had served his country and his God so well. May I only hope that I live the rest of my days in a manner worthy of him.

When I finally reached the Old House after five days of sweltering travel, I entered my father's bedroom. The moment was painful. I was forced to realize that my parents were gone and the enchantment of this house along with them. Yet my attachment to the house and this area remains stronger than ever, and I feel that I must set my own affairs in order and prepare for my retirement.

I have inherited this house and land, and I will retire here to pursue my literary occupations, probably within the next few years. It will be a safe and pleasant retreat, and I would find it repugnant to abandon a place where my father resided for forty years and where I have passed so many happy days.

I was so pleased to note your interest in plants and flowers. I am planning to commence a nursery at the White House in the fall and will want to plant acorns, hickory nuts, and chestnuts.

If you will forgive me, the Creek Indians are not so much on my mind these days.

Your servant,

J. Q. Adams

J. Q. Adams

Thomas Jefferson

Baldwin County, Georgia
To Mr. John Quincy Adams, President
The White House, Washington City
Dear Sir,

I am most appreciative of your last letter and wish that I could add only reinforcement to your thoughts, but now that you must be back in the White House, events in Georgia will not allow me that privilege. Governor Troup has been stirring up trouble again, and most of the planters in this area are egging him on.

What seems most unbelievable is that the governor, in his arrogance, has chosen to ignore the new treaty completely. As soon as the September 1 deadline for surveys under the old Treaty of Indian Springs passed, he sent surveyors into Creek Territory. The rascal wanted to make sure the lands were marked out for sale. Then the Creeks stopped some of the surveyors, and the governor ordered out a troop of cavalry to protect his men!

How awful and illegal are these actions, but that is where matters stand now. I reckon the whole situation presents a web of problems and you are the only one who can do something about them. The least you can do is call off Governor Troup.

Yours respectfully,

Wm. Pratt

Wm. Pratt

P.S. I also do not believe you should be thinking about retiring. You have too many good, productive years ahead of you.

To learn more about Native American lands taken over by the government, visit winslowpress.com.

An engraving of the White House, 1833

Baldwin County, Georgia

To Mr. John Quincy Adams, President

The White House, Washington City

Dear Sir,

To my amazement, I have met Governor Troup! Pa took me. He has known the governor for years.

Because Milledgeville is our capital city, Governor Troup stays there when the legislature is in session. It was a little early for the legislature, but he was in town anyway.

We arrived the night before and stayed at the new three-story tavern, Lafayette Hall. Milledgeville was designed to look like Savannah. It's a checkerboard with a public square on each of the four sides. Lafayette Hall is just north of Statehouse Square and a block from the governor's boardinghouse, which is Mrs. Jenkins'.

We walked up the stairs and knocked on Governor Troup's door. He shouted for us to come in. He was sitting in the middle of the bed in his socks, wearing a beat-up old hat and reading what looked like a book of poetry. He stood up and shook hands, and Pa introduced me. The governor was a short, compact fellow, with deep-set eyes and a sharp jaw.

Almost at once, the governor and Pa were arguing. I could not exactly figure what it was they were arguing about, since they seemed to be on the same side. Then I realized it had to be about the cavalry. Pa thought sending in the cavalry was going too far.

Suddenly Governor Troup started shouting, "Georgia is sovereign on her own soil!" Then he shouted it again.

Pa looked at me, and we left. We shut the door behind us. As we mounted up and started for home, Pa said, "Son, I think it's time the Creek Indians left Georgia."

Sir, you know I do not agree, but something needs to be done.

Yours affectionately,

Wm. Pratt

Wm. Pratt

To learn more about Milledgeville, visit winslowpress.com.

Governor George M. Troup

November 28, 1826

The White House

To Master William Pratt

Baldwin County, Georgia

My dear William,

I am thankful for your word on the troubles in Georgia and deeply disturbed by Governor Troup's decision to call out the cavalry, which must be looked into. I am also astonished at the description of your meeting with the governor.

Had I not been so plagued with visitors and with discussions involving our trade with the West Indies, I would have replied sooner.

On my way back to Washington in mid-October, I had an almost fatal accident. We were about to cross on the ferry from Bristol to Newport when a gale came up. The ferryman felt he could not manage the horse-boat and came over with the sail-boat instead. In the middle of the passage, the waves grew so high that one of our horses lost his footing, reared, and nearly plunged over the side. I was certain that the boat would turn over. When it did not and I was safely on the opposite shore, I had reason to reflect on how slender is the thread of human life, and how incessantly it requires the guardian care of a superior power.

Perhaps, in our frustrating dealings with the governor, we need to rely more on the wisdom of that superior power.

Your servant,

J. Q. Adams

John Quincy Adams

Potomac River in moonlight

December 7, 1826

The White House

To Master William Pratt

Baldwin County, Georgia

My dear William,

I have now given this year's Annual Address, an exercise in futility, I fear. I praised the peace without and the tranquillity within our borders, Georgia notwithstanding. I praised our improvement in foreign trade; though Mr. Anderson died before reaching the Panama conference, Mr. Sergeant set out far too late to get there in time, and I am now contending with Great Britain's decision to ban our trade with the West Indies. My conclusion was best. I paid tribute to the fiftieth anniversary of our independence and those two recently deceased, principal actors in that scene.

If I seemed to be making less of your plight in Georgia than I should have done, believe me, I am not. Governor Troup will be answered in the New Year.

Meanwhile, I continue to walk four miles in the early morning hours, thinking earnest thoughts. I also attend Mrs. Adams's weekly drawing room gatherings and try very hard to be cordial, though my skill at small talk is minimal.

I send best wishes for the holidays, with the grace of God.

Your servant,

J. Q. A.

JQA

To learn more about Mrs. Louisa Adams, visit winslowpress.com.

Louisa Catherine Adams, painting by C.R. Leslie

Baldwin County, Georgia
To Mr. John Quincy Adams, President
The White House, Washington City
Dear Sir,

I understand, yet I am bothered by what is happening with the Creeks. I can find no information about what the cavalry has done. Let us hope that matters are at a standoff, at least for the time being.

School is in recess, and I am doing little walking. I am at home instead, trying to read Cicero and practicing my French. Ma and Sarah and our three house servants are busy at their looms by the fire, weaving cloth to make us new clothes. They work very hard and receive much less credit than they deserve.

I am also trying out my new pair of shoes. Last month a

shoemaker appeared and measured my feet on a plank. Now that the finished shoes have arrived, I am more and more pleased with them.

We are looking forward to the holidays, though thoughts of the indignity of slavery are seldom far from my mind. I would like to discuss this with Paul but know I cannot. It is too dangerous for him to speak his mind.

I send my best holiday wishes to you and Mrs. Adams.

Yours affectionately,

Wm. Pratt

Wm. Pratt

Andrew Jackson and his troops during a Creek rebellion, c. 1815

February 7, 1827

The White House
To Master William Pratt
Baldwin County, Georgia
My dear William,

In the usual fashion, the wheels of government have turned slowly. I have waited to write until I had something to tell you.

It was not until the twenty-seventh of January that I was able to hold a cabinet meeting concerning the problem with the surveyors, the Creeks detaining them, and the Georgia militia. We consulted the act of 1802, which regulated relations with the Indians. It authorized the use of force, and the cabinet recommended that we send in troops.

I did not agree that such an action would be expedient. Before taking up arms, I felt the entire subject should be referred to Congress.

Secretary of War Barbour said he would send an agent to warn the Georgians. I prepared a letter for him to send to Governor Troup. In it, I warned, as politely as possible, that I am charged by the Constitution to carry out the laws and would be forced to use whatever means necessary to carry the new treaty into effect.

I prepared a message for Congress, the most momentous, I felt, that I had ever written, a message delivered just two days ago. In it, I said that if the authorities of the state of Georgia were to persevere in their illegal action, the executive of the United States would be compelled to enforce the laws to the fullest, but only if all other efforts failed.

There the matter rests, at least for the moment.

Your servant,

J. Q. Adams
John Quincy Adams

Etching of John Quincy Adams

Baldwin County, Georgia
To Mr. John Quincy Adams, President
The White House, Washington City
Dear Sir,

I was starting to wonder what had happened. I am pleased that something has, though you will know that I might have preferred a more sweeping sort of action.

I realize that you have acted to protect the new treaty and stand against Governor Troup and his unlawful use of the militia. That is a good thing, but I would be untrue to myself if I did not add that even with order restored, the Indians have been sorely mistreated.

In a more positive spirit, last Sunday Ma gave a quilting bee at our home. Ladies from all over the county came and spent the day sewing their quilts. Mammy Chloe provided a sumptuous feast, and I am proud to say that I was invited to attend.

I thought of it as a little like one of Mrs. Adams's White House receptions, plus quilts.

Yours respectfully,

Wm. Pratt

Wm. Pratt

To learn more about quilting bees, visit winslowpress.com.

An early American quilting bee

March 14, 1827

The White House
To Master William Pratt
Baldwin County, Georgia
My dear William,

Although I do not care for White House receptions, I think I would have liked your mother's quilting bee.

Not that I would have had the time to go. After my address to Congress, in addition to my usual appointments, I worked

very late, often until after midnight, researching the history of our relations with the Indians since the Revolution, the speeches of President Washington, and the journals of the old Congress. I had to conclude that the problem was an unresolved conflict between the rights of the states and the rights of the federal government.

Such a conclusion would have made no difference to your governor. Replying to my letter, he was unrelenting. He wrote, "From the first decisive act of hostility, you will be considered and treated as a public enemy . . . and what is more, the unblushing

Andrew Jackson, the seventh president of the United States, succeeded John Quincy Adams. Shown here (right) in the White House, he enforced the Indian Removal Act of 1830. The Cherokees were forced to march on the "Trail of Tears" to newly created Indian territory west of the Mississippi.

allies of the savages whose cause you have adopted."

As I had requested, Congress took up the subject. The House, where I was about to lose my majority of support after the 1826 elections, declared that it would be best for the United States to purchase title to all Indian lands in Georgia, but that until such time as that became possible, the Treaty of Washington should remain in effect. The already hostile Senate committee, goaded to greater fury by General Jackson's supporters, reported that Georgia already had title to the Creek lands under the Treaty of Indian Springs and could not be attacked by the United States.

Where is the resolution of our concerns? I am afraid there is none. We are in limbo, and I am sorry.

I had wanted a more clearly defined compromise, but with the seating of the new Congress on March 4 and both legislative houses now dominated by the Jacksonian opposition, I have little hope of being heard. Even as I gravitate more toward the Creeks' cause, I seem to have accomplished nothing but a delay that has alienated Georgians and thrown them more completely into General Jackson's camp.

It is inevitable that the Creeks will have to leave. Exactly how soon, I cannot say.

Your servant,

J. Q. Adams

J. Q. Adams

To learn more about the history of the governments relations with Native Americans, visit winslowpress.com.

To learn more about the Creeks' movement westward, visit winslowpress.com.

Baldwin County, Georgia
To Mr. John Quincy Adams, President
The White House, Washington City
Dear Sir,

Last night Paul tried to run away. Pa and James went after him with the hound dogs. All night long, tossing in my bed, I heard the barking. All night long, they searched the riverbank and followed it upstream.

In the morning they brought him back. The dogs had not harmed him, but he was wet and dirty and scratched. He refused to lift his head and look at me.

Pa made him put his arms around the trunk of a big oak tree. He took out the whip and struck him with the lash. When I saw him do that, when I saw the blood run, I could not stand it. I stepped forward, and I grabbed Pa's arm.

I had never stood in Pa's way before, never in all my born days. Pa was the one who made the rules. I was the one who followed them.

Pa looked down at me and glared. He raised his arm again. Then he lowered it and walked away. A few of the other Negroes hurried Paul to the quarters.

I have not seen him today. I hope he is being looked after. Pa has not said there would be any more punishment, so I am hopeful that the incident will be forgotten.

I, however, will not forget. I had never seen anyone whipped before, and it was as if that lash had sliced me open, too. There is no explaining away anything to do with slavery for me anymore.

Can we explain away our treatment of the Indians? Perhaps our Georgia planters and the supporters of General Jackson can, but I cannot do that either.

Yours affectionately,

Wm. Pratt

Wm. Pratt

To learn more about General Andrew Jackson, visit winslowpress.com.

Major General Andrew Jackson, painting by Thomas Sully, c. 1820

June 25, 1827

The White House

To Master William Pratt

Baldwin County, Georgia

My dear William,

I was distressed to receive your last letter and feel badly that my endless round of obligations has delayed my response once again. How horrible it must be to see someone whipped, and how much worse to see someone you know whipped by your own father.

It is true that there is no explaining away the condition of slavery or our removal of the Indians. Perhaps it is only through our belief in God's will and our trust in Him that some small comfort may be drawn.

You will want to know that Colonel Crowell, the Indian agent, has been to see me. He suggests sending soldiers to aid in keeping the peace with the Creeks. Mr. Barbour and I do not believe this move is necessary at the moment, though it has become increasingly clear that the Creeks will have to give up the remainder of their land in Georgia soon.

I have been bathing in the Potomac and passing time each day in the White House garden. My last autumn's plantings have not yet appeared, but I have determined to repeat and multiply the experiments this year. In a space of less than two acres, I have forest and fruit trees, shrubs, hedges, plants, flowers, kitchen and medicinal herbs, and an abundance of weeds.

My drooping health and spirits seem only to be revived by exposure to the natural world.

I trust that you are well and that Paul has recovered.

Your servant,

J. Q. A.

JQA

Several Creeks relax in front of a typical Creek dwelling in Georgia, c. 1790

August 11, 1827

Baldwin County, Georgia
To Mr. John Quincy Adams, President
The Old House
Quincy, Massachusetts
Dear Sir,

We have been enjoying a bountiful summer. The cotton is thriving, along with the corn and the sweet potatoes.

You will be glad to know that Paul has recovered. The wound was deep, but it has healed, leaving a long scar. When I first saw him after that morning at the tree, he thanked me. Since then, we have not spoken of what happened, and neither has Pa. It is probably best that way. What could possibly be said?

I have been thinking more about what you told me about God's will and your own Christian faith. Last week the Methodists came and had a camp meeting in a field near here. The circuit riders are always coming through and sometimes even stay at our house, but this meeting was a real big event and hundreds of people came. They were there all day and all night for a week, exhorting and being exhorted. Three of them jumped up out of a pond and ran about shouting that the devil was after them. They and a number of others got religion. Paul and I just watched. Neither one of us is ready for that kind of religion yet.

Do you think God could do something for the Creek Indians, since nobody else will?

I hope you are feeling better now.

Yours affectionately,

Wm. Pratt

 To learn more about Methodist camp meetings, visit winslowpress.com.

Slaves climbing the steps of a cotton press, sketch by A. R. Waud, printed in Harper's Weekly, 1867

November 28, 1827

The White House

To Master William Pratt

Baldwin County, Georgia

My dear William,

Again, my apologies for the lateness of my reply. Quincy in summer involved me with family and plantings, and now, in Washington City, I appear to be embroiled in endless discussions over questions of politics.

Returning from Quincy in mid-October, I boarded the steamboat Delaware at Philadelphia. Several thousand persons were assembled there, many of them following me onto the boat and thronging the deck until I was able to shake their hands. As the boat left the wharf, three hearty cheers pursued me.

In earlier years, I would have been opposed to these displays of good will from my fellow citizens. I believe they now affect me suitably, since I welcome public support for my views. But even as I hope for that support, I cannot escape the criticism of my friends and colleagues. They continue to insist that I remove political antagonists from their appointments, especially Mr. McLean of the post office, and they demand that I, in the manner of General Jackson's supporters, go out electioneering and exhibiting myself before the people in order to retain my position.

I have neither the heart nor the spirit for these indulgences. Competent officeholders should remain in their posts regardless of their political opinions, and any man interested in the presidency should have that honor bestowed upon him by a grateful public.

Am I a fool to have these thoughts? I feel equally the fool to be compelled to tell you that I have received a letter from

Milledgeville which states that a new treaty, the Treaty of the Creek Indian Agency, has been concluded. In this document, the Creeks have agreed to give up the remainder of their lands within the state of Georgia.

As our great country expands across the continent, we are treating the Indians shamefully and doing them great harm. You may not yet have found your religion, but I know that you will share my view when I say, may God forgive us.

Yours faithfully,

J. Q. Adams

John Quincy Adams

Me-Wa-Wa, a Creek warrior

Baldwin County, Georgia
To Mr. John Quincy Adams, President
The White House, Washington City
Dear Sir,

I am uncertain about the electioneering, but every politician in these parts, Jacksonian or not, seems intent on exhibiting himself before the public at every opportunity.

That seems to be the only way to get elected these days, and I reckon I will have to do it, too.

I have decided to go into politics when I am grown. There is so much that is wrong in our country. Slavery is wrong. Removing the Indians is wrong. Rejecting internal improvements is wrong. I want to go to Congress and help right those wrongs. I want our lives to be different.

I send you and Mrs. Adams warm wishes for the holiday season.

Yours affectionately,

Wm. Pratt

Wm. Pratt

John Quincy Adams: Historical Notes

Young John Quincy Adams

John Quincy Adams was born on July 11, 1767, in the Massachusetts town of Braintree (now called Quincy), into a family that was well-known throughout the New England region. The Adamses were among the original wave of Puritans who had come from England and settled on the Massachusetts South Shore.

John Quincy Adams's father, John Adams, became the second president of the United States in 1797. At the time John Quincy was born, however, John Adams was a bright young lawyer with a keen interest in politics.

John Quincy's mother, Abigail Smith, also came from a prominent New England family. A self-educated woman, she had an intense love of reading. "Johnny," as her eldest son was called, was named after Abigail's grandfather, Colonel John Quincy, one of their town's most distinguished citizens. When John Quincy was one year old, his father moved the family—Abigail, John Quincy, and his older sister Nabby—to Boston. By 1774, they had returned to Braintree, but in the years between, two more children, Charles and Thomas, were born.

John Quincy's early years were lived during a tumultuous time in the history of the United States. Relations between the thirteen American colonies and the British Empire were growing increasingly tense. One of John Quincy's earliest

John Quincy Adams at age 28, portrait by John Singleton Copley, 1795

Attends school in Paris, Amsterdam, and Leyden.	Accompanies Francis Dana to St. Petersburg as private secretary and interpreter for Dana's mission to the court of Catherine the Great.	Leaves Russia to spend winter in Stockholm and Copenhagen.

childhood memories was of climbing with his mother to a promontory across the road from the Adamses' farm and watching the Battle of Bunker Hill unfold before his eyes. These recollections helped shape the private person and public figure that John Quincy was to become.

The elder John Adams became a well-respected leader in opposing the British, but his duties to his country did not prevent him from taking an active role in his children's upbringing. His prosperous law practice—and later, his anti-British activity—frequently kept him away from his family: He was a delegate to the Massachusetts General Court, the defense attorney for the soldiers accused in the Boston massacre (chosen for his high level of integrity, he won the case, sparing the soldiers their lives), and was voted the delegate from Massachusetts to the Continental Congress. Despite being so busy, John Adams maintained constant contact with his wife and children through the many letters they exchanged.

John and Abigail stressed the importance of moral and intellectual excellence to their children. They had a rigorous plan of education for Johnny, who learned Latin, French, and ancient history as early as age seven. John Quincy embraced his parents' demands for scholarly pursuits, and also relished the role of being the "man of the house" when his father was away from home.

Abigail Adams often worried about how John Quincy's responsible nature would affect his behavior. He was a

1783

Rejoins father in Holland and resumes his classical studies. Travels to Paris with father, who has been commissioned (along with Benjamin Franklin and John Jay) to negotiate a peace treaty with Britain.

1785

Returns to United States to attend Harvard College. Graduates with honors in 1787.

1790

Sworn into law practice at age 23.

combative child, quick-tempered, and sensitive to criticism. But he would undertake tasks from which older boys would shy away, determined to be the best at everything he did. This is evident in a letter he wrote to his cousin Elizabeth at the age of six, in which he claimed that he spent "too much of my time in play. There is a great deal of room for me to grow better." At nine, John Quincy took over his absent father's task of riding horseback several miles between Braintree and Boston, carrying the family mail. His father praised him for this accomplishment.

John Quincy's sense of discipline is even more evident in another letter he wrote when he was ten: "I am much more satisfied with myself when I have applied part of my time to some useful employment than when I have idled it away about trifles and play."

In February 1778, John Adams was appointed to a commission in Paris (along with Benjamin Franklin and Arthur Lee) to promote American interests among world powers. It was decided that John Quincy would accompany his father on the trip, and this decision set him on a course that would both enrich and change his life forever.

Life in Europe

John Quincy Adams took full advantage of his years in Europe, quickly mastering the French language. He attended some of the finer schools in Paris, and devoured every bit of

1791

Publishes series of letters under the pen name "Publicola" to refute Thomas Paine's *Rights of Man.*

1794

Appointed minister to Netherlands by President George Washington.

1797

His father, John Adams, becomes the second president of the U.S. Marries Louisa Catherine Johnson on July 26 in London. Appointed minister to Prussia in November.

knowledge they had to offer. He also became more adept socially, and his father commented in several letters to his mother that he was pleased with John Quincy's development. From Braintree, Abigail would write letters to her son pleading with him not to lose his way among the worldly pleasures that Europe had to offer. She was worried that her son would fall under the wrong influences and become a person of low moral character. Over and over again, she urged him to "never disgrace his mother." These letters eventually proved bothersome to the young John Quincy, whose own letters to his mother became fewer and farther between. His father had to keep reassuring his mother that their son was all right.

It was in Paris that young Adams discovered his lifelong attachment to the theater. Contrary to his father's wishes, he developed a love for French comedy and French culture in general.

For the next seven years, John Quincy traveled throughout Europe, first with his father and then on his own, soaking up as much education, culture, and society as possible. He was particularly impressed by Holland and all of its charms. "The frugality, cleanliness, etc. here, deserve the imitation of my countrymen," he wrote in 1780.

In 1781, at the age of fourteen, young Adams was invited to accompany Francis Dana to Russia, serving as his full-time French translator. French was the international language of

1800	1801	1802	1803
Son George Washington Adams is born.	Recalled to United States by father. Opens law office in Boston.	Chosen by Boston Federalists to sit in state senate.	Elected United States senator by the legislature. Second son, John Adams II, is born.

diplomacy at the time, and Dana had been called by the U.S. government to negotiate a treaty with Catherine the Great. After completing his time in Russia, Adams visited family, friends, and connections throughout Europe, and was welcomed at every stop. He enjoyed the attention and lifestyle to such a degree that he often delayed returning to Holland for several months at a time. He had turned fifteen by the time he rejoined John Adams senior and resumed studying under his supervision.

During these years in Europe, John Quincy made the acquaintance of Thomas Jefferson, the minister to France for the U.S. government. Although years older than Adams, Jefferson quickly became a trusted companion. John Quincy remarked in his diary that "I love to be with [Jefferson] because he is a man of very extensive learning and pleasing manners."

Finally, after eight years in Europe, John Quincy returned to the United States to attend Harvard, where his father had gone to college. It was a time of mixed emotions for John Quincy, since he enjoyed both European culture and the company of his father, Jefferson, and Franklin. He knew, however, that returning to the United States would provide him with the opportunity to establish himself on his own terms. At college, he would finally live independently from his overbearing mother and his demanding father.

Elected Boylston Professor of Rhetoric and Oratory at Harvard.

Attends meeting to denounce the sinking of American ship *Chesapeake* by the British ship *Leopard*. Helps draft resolutions and is severed from the Federalists by this act. Third son, Charles Francis, is born.

Resigns as senator. Resumes teaching at Harvard.

Entering Adulthood

John Quincy entered Harvard as a junior and graduated with honors in 1787. It was time to decide what he wanted to do with his future. Once again, he followed in his father's footsteps, choosing to study law and apprenticing himself to Theophilus Parsons of Newburyport.

In 1790, a year after his father took the oath as the nation's first vice president, John Quincy was sworn into law practice and opened his own office in the competitive Boston area. He would later describe his early law career as "four of the most trying years of my life." Business was slow, and John Quincy did not feel that law was his true calling. His father urged him to get involved in local politics, and John Quincy began attending town meetings.

On the strength of several essays written and published in the coming years—including a sound rebuke of Thomas Paine's *The Rights of Man*—John Quincy caught the attention of President George Washington. In May of 1794, with his legal business beginning to prosper, young Adams was appointed minister to the Netherlands. He spent three years there before being appointed minister to Prussia by his father, who was elected president in 1796.

During a trip to London while minister to Prussia, John Quincy met and fell in love with Louisa Catherine Johnson, daughter of the American consul. On July 26, 1797, the two

1809

Appointed minister to
Russia by President
Madison.

1814

Appointed to negotiate
peace between U.S. and
Great Britain at Ghent,
along with four others.
Treaty of Ghent is
signed on Christmas
Eve, ending War of
1812.

1815

Appointed minister
to Britain.

were married. In 1800, while living in Berlin, Louisa gave
birth to their first son, George Washington Adams, named
for the man John Quincy felt was the most influential person
in his life after his father. Three years later, a second son,
John Adams II, was born on the fourth of July. Another son,
Charles Francis, and a daughter, Louisa, would follow in the
coming years. Louisa died while still a baby.

Service to His Country

John Quincy returned to the United States in 1800 and
entered a whirlwind of political activity. He was chosen by
the Boston Federalists to sit in the State Senate in 1802, and
a year later was elected United States senator by the legislature
(the legislature, not the public, voted for congressmen in 1803).
Throughout his tenure as senator, John Quincy would often
disagree with the policies of the Federalist party and vote for
what he believed was in the best interests of the country,
regardless of party concerns. "My sense of duty shall never
yield to the pleasure of a party," he wrote in 1807, after
attending a Republican meeting denouncing the attack on
the American cruiser *Chesapeake* by the British ship *Leopard*.
His ties to the Federalist party were severed after that incident,
and, dejected and disillusioned, he resigned from office later
that year. He resumed private life and taught at Harvard,
where two years earlier he had been appointed Boylston

Professor of Rhetoric and Oratory.

In March of 1809, two days after the new president, James Madison, had taken his oath of office, John Quincy was called in to see him and offered the position of minister to Russia. With his staunch belief that service to one's country should come before all else, John Quincy reluctantly accepted and boarded a ship to Russia with his wife and their two youngest children. It was a difficult decision for Adams because it meant leaving his two older children behind.

In spite of family problems, Adams served successfully in Russia. He then joined four other American diplomats in Ghent, in what is now Belgium, in the spring of 1814 to help negotiate peace with Britain and put an end to the War of 1812. After some trying negotiations, a peace treaty was signed on Christmas Eve 1814 that was passed unanimously by Congress, concluding what Adams called "the most memorable year of my life." Madison then appointed John Quincy minister to Great Britain, where the Adams family spent the next two years.

In 1817, John Quincy received a letter from newly elected President James Monroe informing him of his appointment as secretary of state. Eight years after leaving Boston at a low ebb in his career, John Quincy Adams returned to a warm reception. His tenure as secretary of state was one of the most successful political periods of Adams's life. He would greatly contribute to America's westward expansion, establish the

| Nominated for presidency. | Wins presidential election despite losing popular vote. Is elected by House of Representatives. | Father, John Adams, dies. |

Monroe Doctrine in foreign policy, and put himself in a strong position to succeed Monroe as president.

The Election of 1824

The presidential election of 1824 was both chaotic and controversial. The Federalists could offer no candidate, and as a result, there were no party affiliations. There were five candidates, one of whom was Adams. When no one received a majority of the electoral vote, the House of Representatives had to choose the winner from among the top three finishers: Adams, Andrew Jackson (who had won the popular vote by 30,000 ballots), and William Crawford. Kentucky's Henry Clay narrowly missed being the third candidate.

On February 9, 1825, the House of Representatives met to elect the sixth president of the United States. On the first ballot, with the northern states going to Adams and the southern states split between Crawford and Jackson, the Clay-influenced western states of Kentucky, Ohio, Louisiana, and Missouri gave their votes to Adams. With only thirteen states needed at that time to win a majority of the House, the votes of New York, Illinois, and Maryland secured the election. When Adams later announced the appointment of Clay as secretary of state, an outraged Jackson voiced the opinion of many by declaring the election a "corrupt bargain" between Adams and Clay. Adams's reaction to the outcome was never publicly proclaimed, but was recorded in his diary. The

1828

Loses race for reelection to
Andrew Jackson.

1830

Elected by landslide margin to the House
of Representatives from Massachusetts.
Becomes first ex-president to serve in
Congress after his presidency. Would
serve in the House until his death.

election, he wrote, was not "in a matter satisfactory to pride
or to just desire; not by the unequivocal suffrages of a majority
of the people." It was the beginning of an unpopular and
contested presidency, widely viewed as the low point of
Adams's political career.

Adams's Presidency and the Creek Indians of Georgia

Adams's opponents began their onslaught from the moment
he took office, and they never let up. His first Annual Address
was viewed as highly unpopular and out of touch with the
American public, although his proposals, which included a plan
for widespread internal improvements and a commitment to
the arts and sciences, can be viewed in hindsight as ahead of
their time. A second major contributing factor to Adams's
failed presidency was his hesitancy to promote his own ideas.
Intent on not getting caught up in political maneuvering, he
would not fire the cabinet members who opposed him and
replace them with his own supporters. This sent the message
throughout Washington that it was acceptable to oppose
the presidency and unrewarding to support it—a lethal
political combination.

The Creek Indian situation was another problem. Soon
after he entered office, Adams ratified the Treaty of Indian
Springs between the state of Georgia and the Creek Indians,
in which the Creeks agreed to hand over their territorial

Delivers eulogy for President
Monroe in Boston.

Is seized by a stroke and collapses at
his desk in the House. Dies two days
later, on February 23.

rights to the state. Unbeknownst to Adams, the treaty was
the result of a bribe made to a Lower Creek chief, William
McIntosh, by state and federal officials. The Upper Creeks
saw the treaty as fraudulent, killed Chief McIntosh after
he signed it, and refused to give up their land. Georgian
surveyors, with the full support of their Governor Troup,
were already laying claim to that land.

Adams had never been a vocal supporter of the Indian
cause in the past, but his attitude had softened over the years.
He and his cabinet agreed to halt implementation of the first
treaty and renegotiate. This infuriated Governor Troup. Even
after a second treaty had been signed, he ignored the official
word from Washington and continued to move his men onto
Creek land, where the Creeks were challenging any land
surveyor who entered their territory. Try as he might, Adams
could not find a solution to the matter because of the mag-
nitude of Georgia's resistance, which was backed by old Indian
fighter and Adams enemy Andrew Jackson. It was obvious
that Jackson's supporters in Congress, of which there were
many, would not agree to a more equitable treaty. With
tensions at their highest, a third treaty was forged at the last
minute, in which the Creeks finally agreed to surrender all
their remaining land in Georgia. Despite the Georgia victory,
Adams's interference in the matter was a cause for much
resentment toward him in the South.

Adams did not enjoy his presidency. The responsibilities—constant meetings, listening to petitioners for office, attending social events—did not suit his bookish personality, and he became easily bored with his duties. He also became disenchanted with the growing partisan politics of the time.

With his unsuccessful first term coming to an end, Adams ran for reelection in 1828 against Andrew Jackson. The contest was marked by the first appearance of the "smear campaign" in presidential elections. The candidates' supporters hurled defamatory remarks at one another, most of which were untrue. Adams was accused of offenses such as marrying a woman not born in the United States (Louisa was an American born in Great Britain), opposing the Louisiana Purchase (which he had not), and spending public funds for a pool table and chess set for the White House. Adams's supporters countered by rehashing Jackson's duels and brawls on the frontier and charging that he was illiterate. They also accused him of stealing his wife from another man and then living with her out of wedlock for many months. This charge, another distortion of the real circumstances, infuriated Jackson. He blamed his wife's death shortly after the election on his political enemies.

Jackson won by a large margin in the electoral college, but the popular vote was much closer. Adams left office greatly depressed. He wrote that the election left his "character and reputation a wreck" and that the sun of his political life "sets in the deepest gloom."

Little did he know that his next career, as a staunchly antislavery congressman, would open up to him in 1830. It would last until his death in 1848.

Home and Family

Louisa Adams was an attractive woman who enjoyed the arts, played the harp and piano, sang, wrote poetry, and acted as a fine hostess. Her marriage, however, was not a happy one. In an autobiography she wrote at the end of John Quincy Adams's presidency, Louisa portrayed herself as a bitter woman who resented her husband's lofty ambitions. Guilt-ridden about having been separated from her two oldest boys during her time in Russia, she suffered from numerous nervous ailments. She stopped accompanying John Quincy on the trips he made back to the family home in Quincy from August to October each year, and she despised living in the yet-to-be-renovated White House, which she called "a dull and stately prison."

To quench his growing dissatisfaction during his time as president, John Quincy Adams turned to the more leisurely pursuits of gardening and astronomy. He planted an extensive garden on the White House grounds and also installed a telescope on the roof. He spent hours in the garden each day, planting thousands of seedlings, some of which were imported from overseas.

John Quincy Adams was just as hard and demanding on his children as he was on himself, and as his own parents had been on him. His oldest son, George Washington Adams, did not respond well to this pressure. He was brilliant but unstable, had problems with alcohol, and had difficulty facing John Quincy's disappointment in his escapades. On a steamboat home to Washington at the end of his father's presidency, George jumped overboard and drowned. He was twenty-eight years old.

John Adams II, once forbidden by his father to come home from Harvard for Christmas because he was doing poorly in his studies, was eventually expelled from the college for helping to incite a riot. His father forgave him and appointed him his presidential personal secretary in 1824. John would later marry Mary Hellen, one of the three orphaned children of Louisa's sister. They lived in the White House with Louisa and John Quincy. Like his brother George, John also died young, falling into a coma in 1834, a victim of apparent overwork and possibly alcoholism.

Charles Francis was the only son to live up to his parents' expectations, becoming minister to Great Britain and, with a talent for financial management, eventually taking over the family's estate.

Books written for kids

Bial, Raymond. *The Cherokee*. New York: Marshall Cavendish, 1998.

Bealer, Alex W. *Only the Names Remain: The Cherokees & the Trail of Tears*. Boston: Little, Brown, 1996.

Kent, Zachary. *John Quincy Adams*. Danbury, CT: The Children's Press, 1987.

Walker, Jane C. *John Quincy Adams*. Springfield, NJ: Enslow, 2000.

Books that kids and adults can enjoy

Williams, Jeanne. *Trails of Tears: American Indians Driven from Their Lands*. Dallas: Hendrick-Long, 1992.

Nagel, Paul C. *John Quincy Adams*. Boston: Harvard University Press, 1997.

Nevins, Allan. *The Diary of John Quincy Adams*, 1794-1845. New York: Charles Scribner's Sons, 1951.

Parsons, Lynn H. *John Quincy Adams*. Madison, WI: Madison House Publishers, 1998.

Here is a reproduction of an actual letter from John Quincy Adams to Thomas Jefferson, written on November 18, 1824.

William Pratt's letters might have looked something like this:

March 23, 1825

To John Quincy Adams, President
The White House
Washington City

Dear Sir,
I have learned that about two weeks ago,
you signed a treaty with the Creek Indians
called the treaty of Indian Springs. It says
that the Creeks would give up all their land
here in Georgia. They would have to move to
an equal amount of land west of the
Mississippi River and receive a bonus
of $400,000. I do not think this is fair
at all.
Yours Respectfully,
Wm. Pratt

In this book, William Pratt sent his letters to President Adams via the U.S. Postal Service. Sending a letter in those days was much different from sending one today. In the beginning of the nineteenth century, envelopes were not used. Instead, each letter was folded with the address written on the outside. Most letters were delivered to and picked up from the post office. Since William had no post office nearby, he had to use the closest stagecoach stand instead. Mail was only delivered directly to a person's home by a carrier in the major cities of the United States, for an additional charge of a penny or two.

Stamps as we know them were not used until 1847. In 1825, postal charges were based on the number of miles a letter traveled and the number of sheets the letter contained rather than on its weight. Single-sheet letters that traveled more than 400 miles—as was the case with William and President Adams's correspondences—cost twenty-five cents! This practice began in 1816 and lasted until 1845. Letters were generally sent with the postage unpaid, since it would be collected from the addressees. It was the exception for the person writing the letter to pay the postage up front. Prepayment of postage was not made mandatory until thirty years later, in 1855.

By 1825, stagecoaches carrying mail were making the trip from Washington, D.C., to the southern states on approximately eleven-day schedules. In 1823, Congress designated all navigable waters as postal routes, allowing mail to travel by steamboat as well.

More information on the history of the United States Postal Service can be found online at http://www.usps.gov/history.

Interactive Web Footnotes

Here is an alphabetical list of the interactive footnotes found at the bottom of the pages in this book. We hope that this list will prove to be an easy reference for locating the subjects you are interested in at this book's own Web site at **winslowpress.com**.

Index

(Colored numbers represent photographs and illustrations)

A

B

Etching of John Quincy Adams

C

D

E

F

G

H

I

J

L

M

O

P